SEVEN
SKIES

SEVEN SKIES

Niraj Doshi

PARTRIDGE
A Penguin Random House Company

To order additional copies of this book, contact
Toll Free 800 101 2657 (Singapore)
Toll Free 1 800 81 7340 (Malaysia)
orders.singapore@partridgepublishing.com

www.partridgepublishing.com/singapore

To mom, dad and that beautiful childhood......

STORIES

THE CURSE OF COOBER PEDY

"I don't believe our lives have any purpose. Being born is just a chance event and then destiny leads us, wherever…" – Merv Ian McGregor

1979 Australasia

The eyes open to a red sky. Not the soft amber of a setting sun, but the visceral red of fresh blood. Merv bats his eyelids, half-expecting to see the bedroom ceiling. But, inflamed clouds stare back at him.

"HITLER! Stop it …" – he kicks the pug.

It moves away from his foot and starts licking the forehead, instead. Merv tries to gulp air by the mouthful. The sleep has left him breathless. A cigarette – naah, a friggin' cigar would be great to clear off the head. He's quit but then technically, a cigar is not a cigarette. And anyways how would mom know? He slides a hand towards the hip pocket for a light, but bare skin greets his sweaty palm.

"That's interesting, my dear Watson…." "I, Merv the great McGregor and you Hitler the douchebag doggy wake up bang in the middle of this street. That too, stark naked!"

Wish Lucia was here. They'd smoke a joint and all this would seem meaningful. Propping up on his elbows, he scans the arid landscape. The dirt track is bereft of any movement. Coober Pedy resembles a ghost-town most evenings. Even at its busiest during Sunday market, this settlement of thousand odd is hardly a beehive. And the population continues to dwindle, year on year.

"The Curse of Coober Pedy..." – he wiggles his finger at Hitler, imitating Fr. Braganza.

"Woorf…"

He kneels down and caresses its auburn fur. A scar, jagged and thick, begins above its eye and disappears into the hairline.

"Holy dooly! What's that goog?"

A mangled layer of skin flaps in place of the missing ear. He closes his eyes, trying to rewind the past few hours. Or is it days?

"MERV…" – mom's shriek echoes in his mind.

There's no visual to go with it. It's as if somebody has clean-slated a part of his life.

He shuts his ears as the evening siren blares from the mines. Billowing smoke dissolves into the bloodied sky but there's no sign of Uncle Joey and his motley band of opal scavengers. Even, the cattle station is barren. He stares at a solitary emu lurking afar. Hadn't the species gone extinct in this part of the Outback? What else would this God-damned place throw up!

A century back this was a nameless, shapeless piece of land inhabited by Aboriginals. And then someone chanced upon opal and started digging away. Nameless, shapeless became Kupa Piti, the white man's hole. Coober Pedy was the bastardized, anglicized version. *"More like a shit hole."* – *he used to crib to Lucia.*

He thrusts upright in his favorite Jean Claude Van Damme style. Hitler mimics his jump, trying to catch its own tail.

"Stupid biiiitch!"

He eyeballs the shattered sign-board ahead. Fluorescent marks gleam besides it, shapes unclear in the fading light.

"Merv…Merv" – a voice emanates from the church.

He's heard the voice before, gravelly as if laced with soot. He palms his ears, but it drowns down.

"Ok girl, let's nick off."

Recent incidents have rattled everyone, especially after the accidental death of 5 miners. *"Their spirits will not rest till they find peace"* – *the superstitious lot had proclaimed.*

They scuttle towards the dugouts - underground residences built through an ancient cave to thwart nature's vagaries.

The desert oak outside their home arcs against the gust, but he doesn't feel an iota of breeze. Confetti and deflated balloons flutter all over the lawn. Party? Yes of course, his birthday. Is it today? A placard on the mailbox catches his attention. He squints to decipher mom's writing.

House on Sale. Urgent – Price Negotiable

"Yay! What a birthday gift…"

An airplane tears through the cloud cover.

"Hell to Hollywood." – he winks at Hitler and gestures at himself and then at the plane.

He glances at the row of empty dugouts. *Where is everyone?* He hops down the front porch and is about to ring the bell. The door opens on its own but nobody comes out.

"Mom?" – he tip-toes into the living room.

The vacant sofa seat is reclined and compressed. A Chardonnay bottle smashes on the floor and poodles of burgundy spread out. He bites his lips and looks around the room. The portrait behind the sofa has them huddled together. A crack runs across the glass, right across pop's face. It's been five years since he deserted them. Time heals they say. Not if the wounds were from the summer of 1974.

Laughter of spring warmed the house. Mom was the life of those weekend gatherings. She cooked amazing meat pies and tap-danced with every friend of pop, no matter how drunk or daft he might be. And deep into the night, pop would regale us with stories from around the world. He was a voracious reader and the mines of Coober Pedy couldn't hold back his imagination.

But then, something changed. The heat of summer dried up the land – our parties stopped abruptly. People no longer visited. Pop kept to himself, returning late every night. And every once in a while he'd make Merv repeat the promise.

"Yes, I'll take care of mom. I promise." - he whispers.

The recent quibbles had challenged his resolve. He'd decided to leave Australia, with or without her. But tonight he yearns to see her toothy smile. The clock chimes 12 times and shows 12th December. 12th December!

"Happy Birthday to me… happy …" "Mom?!" – he peeps down the stairway hoping for her to spring up in surprise.

On one such birthday, pop gave him the best and worst surprise of his life. A pup with a wrinkly, short-muzzled face sat on his tummy, that morning. The glossy coat covered a compact body with well-developed muscle. He fell in love with its button ears, but love is only hatred not yet discovered. Pop vanished that evening to never come back. That's when he named the pug, Hitler.

"Careful…"

Hitler skirts around the glass shards and jumps onto the sofa.

He squats at the fireplace extending his palms over the logs. The flames growl without any warmth. A photo floats by and falls into the fire.

"What …" - he swirls.

The room is still deserted. Lucia's eyes glow in the fire, the remainder face charred as her photo burns. He notices the ashtray on the windowsill. A half-lit cigarette simmers through a long finger of ash. Some images from yesterday flood in.

Cigarette balanced between fingertips, mom snuggled in the rocking chair. She sipped on her evening quota of wine, probably her fourth glass.

"You…you can't go out with Lucia tomorrow."

"Who are you do decide that, Mom? It's my life."

"She's too rash for you…"

"Living life in the fast lane isn't rash. You won't understand." – he threw the pullover she'd woven for his birthday.

The photo-frame fell and cracked on impact. Pop's face cut into two.

"Merv, don't say that…"Please…please come back."

He stormed out. Mom's wayward footsteps followed. Hitler loped along, tugging hard at his jeans.

Blank. He can't remember anything beyond.

He walks over to the dining table. His favorite oats pancake with maple syrup lie untouched. He's about to call the sheriff when boisterous laughter arises from the living room. He hops over, only to find the grainy tape of his first birthday playing on screen. The remote is suspended on the edge of the sofa. His heart wells up looking at the video, which shows him wobbling towards pop on Bondi beach. Pent-up rage gives way to tears which do not flow. The only mistake he ever did was to leave. And this one error upturned more than a decade of bliss. Suddenly, the TV shuts off.

"This is not funny, mom!"

One by one, the glass pieces and wine stains vanish from the floor. Hitler hides behind the sofa.

"C'mon, did you find anything downstairs?" – he skips down the rickety stairs.

His bedroom is altered beyond recognition. It's as if a giant vacuum cleaner sucked it off all life. Nothing in the room suggests that anyone ever lived here. No posters, no books, no video cassettes. The sole survivor is a mattress. His photographs are strewn all over, except in the center.

One photo rises from top of the pillow and blows out the window. He peeks outside, fearing that he might see her body. He releases his grip on Hitler's neck as the backyard is empty.

"Do you think mom's also left us?"

He turns to search for the torch, but his cupboard is empty. The figurine of Jesus on top is illuminated by a candle.

After pop left, she became a bit barmy and even attempted suicide once. She took up drinking with a vengeance. In retaliation he stopped attending Sunday mass. Anyways what help had being religious served his parents? Bit by bit disdain converted to nonchalant non-belief. He concluded that God was just a figment of man's imagination. Only weaklings needed this concept to overcome their fears and manage their destinies.

'Please keep mom safe…' – Ironically his heart sends out a silent prayer. To whom, he did not know.

He hears a car zip by, and a thud booms in his memory. *He was crossing the dirt track, followed by mom. She faltered, trying to push him away as the car screeched to a halt.*

He darts out of the house and traces the bigger fluorescent mark on the street – a human outline. Mom? Hope she's alive. Can those bizarre statements she used to dish out actually be true?

'The curse of Coober Pedy holds back the spirits.' 'The dead are living till they release themselves.'

A light goes off in the house.

"Hitler, someone's there. Quick – let's get in."

As they enter the house, the door closes on them and the latch comes up. Till this moment, he didn't believe in spirits, but as Fr. Braganza used to say that there comes a time in life, when all our beliefs turn on their head.

And now for the first time, he feels like a foolish teenager who's clueless about life. It is no longer about the rage against pop, the on-off status with Lucia or the yearning to run away from the outback. Life is taking a strange turn today – he has turned 18 and his entire belief system is being questioned.

"Mom…" – unformed tears refuse to drop off the dry eyes.

"No no no, let's not imagine things."

He ransacks every room, piece of furniture, corner of the house. The back door to the verandah flings open. He treads on the week-old grass, keeping his eyes on the ground.

"Merv…" – the gravelly voice calls him again.

The bell-tower booms and they sprint towards the church. As they approach the gate, he sees two figures wandering in the adjacent graveyard. A couple of graves have been dug afresh.

One of the naked men strides towards him. Merv curses himself for forgetting to get into some clothes. Fresh lilies adorn the grave where they come face to face. Merv extends his hand, but to his discomfort, the old man embraces him. He's unnaturally strong for his age. The freckled face looks familiar.

"Howdy lad?"

"Do I know you, sir?"

"Aye and Nay"

"What's that supposed to mean?"

"That's immaterial my boy. The more important question is what are you looking for?"

"Have you seen a middle-aged lady – thick glasses, shoulder length hair…"

"Hang on. I didn't ask who, but what?"

"Look mister, I don't really have time for this …."

"Hmmm…c'mon kiddo, isn't it fun? Thrashing out the mysteries of life by asking the right questions."

"FUN?! My mom is missing, possibly d…ddead. Psychological mumbo-jumbo is hardly fun for me. Not now, infact never."

The old man gives a toothless smile and comes closer – pop in older age, would've probably looked like him.

"Alright, lemme ask you a couple of questions and then I'll tell you where your mother is."

"Ok, shoot."

"What's your calling in life?"

"Hmm…Eat, drink and enjoy till I'm like you and then lie down in one of these" – he points to the graves with irritation.

"And after that?" – the old man sits down on one of the graves.

"What do you mean?"

"Everyone has a purpose for his or her existence"

"I don't believe our lives have any purpose. Being born is just a chance event and then destiny leads us, wherever…"

"But you do not cease to exist, until you fulfill your destiny either in this life, or the after-life."

"So what's yours, sir?"

"Reconciling a broken family and liberating my son from his sorrow."

Merv shudders as the old man's body starts evaporating.

"Your mother is just besides you. Feel her presence." – the words come out before the last remnants of the man are gone.

Fresh footmarks get engraved in the wet soil. The invisible feet must belong to someone petite, feminine.

A dark silence engulfs the surroundings. The younger man who till now was standing at a distance, comes closer. Red clouds block the moonlight and his face isn't visible clearly. The man signals Merv to move closer to the inscription on the grave.

'R.I.P.

In loving memory of my children

Merv Ian McGregor & Hitler

Born 12/12/1962

Died 11/12/1979'

Suddenly pain floods his brain. He squirms, yanking his burning foot away from Hitler. He squeezes his temples and a lump of tissue falls off his forehead.

Mom tried pushing him away but stumbled on the lawn. He looked behind as she shrieked "MERV…"

He saw the scared eyes of Lucia in the driver's seat as the Wrangler rammed into him and Hitler. As they lay on the middle of the road, transiting from the state in between life and death he saw the vehicle zip by.

"Merv." – the gravelly voice looms large now.

"Pop!"

His shoulders start trembling and the pain vibrates through every cell of his body.

"Welcome son. May our souls rest in peace."

"Where's mom?"

"Julia is safe. Lilies are still a favorite, eh?" - Pop points to the footmarks.

"Tell me all this is a lie, please…We're still alive, right?"

"Why fear death, sonny? Just because you don't know what it is… But then again who really knows what life is? Maybe, just a dead man's illusion!"

Blurry pictures reel in his mind; his 17 year old life running backwards. There's a pause at the evening when he'd last seen pop – a black cap, hiding his balding pate.

"Why did you leave us?"

"Merv, I left because my time was up and I didn't want both of you suffering my cancer too."

"And what about the hatred we lived through!"

"Sorry son. Maybe that's why my body died but the spirit survived…" "The curse of Coober Pedy is actually a blessing in disguise. You get a chance even after death."

Merv drops down on his knees and looks at the parting clouds. The soft amber of a rising sun replaces the blood red sky. The three of them start evaporating. He feels liberated as he hugs Hitler, still licking at his dried-out wounds.

> *'Just as no one can be forced into*
> *belief, so can no one be forced into unbelief.'*
> *- Sigmund Freud*

HALLUCINATIONS OF AMBITION

"I smell a mutiny. And that means death for a
whole bunch of you lazy bastards" – Cook

18th Century: Southern Ocean/
2051: Asia, Antarctica

*Against choppy waters, HMS Resolution rocks like a
Babushka doll. I wedge myself against the starboard railing.
Skin peels off my blistered fingers.*

*"Damn you!" – I spit into the ocean, as a wave taller than
the pyramids crashes in.*

*Darkness traps us from every direction. Only intermittent
lightning helps distinguish the gurgling ocean from the opened
up sky. But we can't turn back. Not a third time. Not this
time!*

*I drag myself to the ship's rear, towards the source of those
screams. The boys are leaning over the stern.*

"ROGER…. Hang on…." – Pike throws in a buoy.

*I recollect ordering Roger to repair the cant frame an hour
back. They throw in another float but there's no way he can be
rescued. His flapping hands are no longer visible.*

*"Get the boys in, Pike. And lock the decks!" – I holler over
the gale.*

"Aye aye Captain."

Fourth life in as many months.

*I walk over to the bridge. Clerke is at the wheel. I check
his log. It shows we've crossed 50° 53' S. Still a bloody long
way to go.*

"Any news from Captain Furneaux?"

Clerke spreads his feet for balance, as the ship nosedives.

"No sir, we've lost all contact with HMS Adventure."

"Fire the light guns every hour, and keep me informed."

"Aye aye…. ABC." – a squeaky voice erupts from behind.

As I turn, sixty pairs of giggling eyes stare back. Water from the windowsill drips onto my brow. Outside the room, Kolkata's sewage water replaces the ocean of my hallucination. What stared off as sporadic childhood dreams have now grown up into frequent adulthood embarrassments.

I adjust my glasses. The auditorium of St. Anne's high school is a collision of two distinct worlds – 3D projectors and CCTVs interlaced with half-eaten food particles and plastic roaches.

"OK girls, this is the 7th continent." – I point to Antarctica on the virtual globe.

The contours seem familiar. Inviting. Hopefully, I'll get on the December cruise and the white wilderness will unlock the mysteries, as well as miseries of my life.

The bell reverberates.

"Thank you, teacher!" – the fifth graders shout in unison.

A stray "ABC" is murmured in between.

"Mr. Cook, please!" – my plea drowns amidst peals of young laughter as a paper missile hits my forehead.

Mr. Akhouri Byron Cook. Who would ever take such a name seriously?

Wonder what made my great grand-father stay back in India, post the demise of the East India Company. Of course, apart from the Bengali danseuse he'd rescued from a mental asylum. And now a century later here I was, the result of that doomed matrimony. A Brit face stuck on an Indian tummy, teaching geography to girls who hadn't yet hit puberty.

If only he'd returned to Essex then. If only I could get to MIT. If only Victoria had settled down in India. If only life could re-run on all my ifs.

I scoot off the alley, ready to take on my next challenge. Dr. Dhingra.

*　　*　　*

I lie on the couch, hoping not to doze off like last time. The cold room feels anti-septic and anti-logic.

"Breathe…. Focus…." – Dr. Dhingra's nasal tone grates my nerves.

But with each exhalation I feel lighter.

"Feel your face loosening."

My muscles relax progressively - beginning with the jaws, down the neck, shoulders, back and legs. My body sinks into the couch.

"Can you visualize a bright light around your forehead?"

"Yes."

"Imagine the light spread down every muscle, nerve, organ. Let the light fill your being and surround it as well."

"Ten….Nine…Eight…."

"Ektho"

Click.

I am falling down an unending tunnel. All background noises ebb.

"How old are you?"

"Ten"

"What do you see?"

"Sea?…naa, a lake. Salt lake of Kolkata"

"Are you swimming?"

"Just standing - at the edge of a ramp. I don't know how to swim."

"There's a push from behind, and I feel my leg slip."

"The boys are laughing …garrr"

"Water…my lungs…..Help….garrr…"

"Suddenly my choking stops. The arms are gliding on the surface, chopping through the ripples."

"I'm swimming now, effortlessly. As if I've always lived in and around water."

"Stop. You're out now. It's a new day" "Go back further in time. Even before you were born."

"Shhhh….Quiet. See those?"

"What?"

"White Boulders of Death."

"What do you see?"

"SHUT UP! And get back to work, you fools!"

"Pass pass pass…." – Clerke shouts as two crew members dribble with a rock of ice.

The fog is clearing up. I glare at the sea of ice, punctuated by massive bergs in the horizon. If only my stare could thaw these. Icicles frost along the flattened sails.

"Captain, one more down to scurvy"- Pike rushes up the stairway.

I lick salt off an ice chunk. We hoisted several of these yesterday. A ton worth of fresh water.

"Where are we on supplies?"

"Only few sacks of biscuits left, sir."

"Cabin C?"

"Onions, beef, fruits… all ransacked by rats" "Should we turn North?"

"No, let's ply on."

"But captain…"

"Concentrate on your bloody work and leave the decision making to me!"

We are too close to turn back now. Not after thousand miles and two years of near misses. There has to be a major landmass somewhere down south. And I'll be the first to discover it.

"Captain, a 5 knot headwind is pushing back. Also the ice field is damaging the keel."

"Turn the sail. Let's try to break through the east."

Dr. Bronson trudges in.

"We need to head back." - his eyes are bloodshot.

"What's the matter, Bronson?"

"James, you've already lost four men and this can't…."

Pike moves to the corner, pretending to be immersed in his journal.

"James? James! It's Captain Cook."

I pull Bronson by the collar. His shirt stenches of brandy.

"And now you've started drinking during duty hours?"

"Let go. You're back."

I open my eyes to a calm Dr. Dhingra. I release his coat and walk out to the foyer.

"Was I back there, doctor?"

"Yes, the same old ship!"

"Can I get the transcripts?"

"Sure, but they won't be accurate. You didn't speak out half the time - it was as if you were possessed."

"So, what do you think?"

"I need to consult a couple of colleagues. Let's meet next month."

I escape the clinic with more questions than answers. This psychedelic past-life regression is in the realms of non-scientific bozos. How Dhingra calls himself a doctor is a mystery in itself. But at least ma will be off my back.

I check emails on my iNano. The cruise confirmation is in. I grin at the kids playing soccer in the rain, as my scooty zips by.

'Antarctica beckons, sweetheart. Pack your bags' – I message Victoria.

*   *   *

We've crossed 60° 40' S and are clocking 10 nautical miles an hour. A pod of hump-backs squirt water in the distance. Days stop turning into nights as the sun hovers lazily across the horizon.

The gale has abated but temperatures continue to plummet as we ply further south. Sleet on the rigging ornaments the ship outline.

I enter her dank cabin. Sickness has spread its tentacles to every corner. She's wrapped under a layer of blankets.

"James?" – her voice wheezes with phlegm.

"Shhhh…"

"Are we on our way back?"

"This is our best chance at greatness, my precious. Bronson will get you fit and floating."

Her lips part weakly and she pulls my ear to her bloated tummy.

I feel a kick. A tiny sailor ready to set sail.

"Rose, I…"

"Rose from your slumber, my dumb and dumber"

"Urgh ma…!" – soaked in sweat, I push off the blankets.

"Lazy bwoy" – ma strokes my receding hairline. "Shouldn't you start packing?"

The iNano vibrates.

"Fatso!"

"Hey Ms. DNA, what's up?"

I snuggle into a ball holding the pillow between my legs. That's the effect Victoria's voice has on me. It's like chicken soup for my deranged soul.

"You still haven't sent across your latest blood sample!"

"MITians are worse than the blood-sucking mosquitoes of Kolkata." "How many bottles have you dunked, so far? My mom thinks you were a vampire in your last birth."

"Ouch" – ma thwacks my head.

"HA HA! Funny doesn't suit you, Fatso. See you at Ushuaia."

"Any answers for the hallucinations?"

"Nearly there. I promise a conclusion before we set foot on your wet dream."

"Ok. Ciao."

Ma ruffles my hair and starts folding the blankets.

"Akhu, I've booked an appointment with Dr. Dhingra on your return."

"I'm not going to waste any more time with that dodo. Hypnosis, re-birth, that's all bullshit."

"So, what makes you think, your Victoria has all the answers?"

"How can you compare her to that quack? Victoria is a genetic scientist working in the most advanced research lab in the world."

"And you are her lab rat."

"Hey ma!" - I lay prostrate and hold her feet.

With the backing of her 330 million Hindu Gods, she thinks the re-incarnation theory is unbeatable. Especially, after Apollo Hospital ruled out Multiple Personality Disorder, Schizophrenia and other infamously famous mental conditions.

But, my heart says Victoria will crack the conundrum. She was my alter-ego at university, where she'd joined us as an exchange student from Boston. We haven't met for the past 5 years, but are in touch on a weekly basis. She's been prodding me to re-apply for masters at the Geosciences department of MIT. Third time lucky, maybe.

*   *   *

I finish packing and email the latest hallucinations transcripts to Victoria. Excitement, nervousness and adrenalin keep my mind racing through the night. Just when my eyes begin to droop, a cuckoo blares on the banyan tree outside. It's already 5 am. The first rays of dawn stream through as I fumble for the lamp. I stare at the antique map covering half the ceiling. The year 1773 is scribbled on it. I doodle in the air, tracing a line which doesn't seem a part of the original map. Scrawled as if an afterthought, it starts from Plymouth in UK all the way to New Zealand and circumventing back from above Antarctica. I remember seeing this path in my dreams.

I wash my face and put on the floppy hat hanging behind the bathroom door. I'd bought it along with the map from the antique bazaar.

I'm admiring my bushy mustache, when suddenly a face replaces mine. A cold wave runs down my spine. The mirror reflects a weather-beaten, bearded man. But the hat is the same. I've seen him before. But where? I squeeze my eyes shut to narrow down the memory hunt. Where, where, where? Goosebumps spread over my naked torso. It's him. The captain from my hallucinations.

I fling the hat and scamper back to the bedroom. I tread to the closet and pick up my bags. The wardrobe mirror reflects someone. Through the corner of my eye, I notice a paunch. I stand upright and face the fear. Thankfully this time, the familiar rotund face of Akhouri Byron Cook reflects back.

The journey to the airport is uneventful. Ma thankfully agreed to stay at home, instead of creating a scene at the new Dum Dum international terminal.

*   *   *

I nestle into the economy seat of Air India, which is marginally bigger than their commode. The flight info suggests we'd be flying over the Pacific en-route to Buenos Aires.

Ting tong, ting tong – the kid besides me mimics the attendant call button. Across the aisle, a toddler wails whilst its parents steal a smooch. As soon as the wheels rumble along the tarmac, sari-clad airhostesses start miming the deaf-and-dumb game of safety.

I down a miniature Kilbeggan – the world's oldest whisky brand. I'm surprised these guys stock such exquisite stuff! Sounds muffle up before eventually dying down, as I burrow under the shawl.

Nobody's around - I swig down the last drop of Kilbeggan from the flask. Every sinew of my body is aching. Sixth month at sea with God knows how many more to go.

Ice structures pack in together forming an impenetrable fortress. A similar float lies to the South-East, no end to it visible from the mast-head. Flocks of red-billed arctic terns soar over the bergs. But we are locked for the time being.

"Bronson, how's Rose?"

"Better. But we need to move ashore to ensure a safe delivery."

I press a button to summon Pike.

"Yes sir" - a feminine voice rings in my ear.

Surprisingly it's Rose who walks over to the cabin. Her eyes look tired, but the lip gloss is alive. She's wearing a kitschy uniform over her corset.

"Rose?"

"Sir." – she shakes my shoulder. My eyes are wide open now. "Please fasten your seatbelt, we're about to land."

The shorter flight from Buenos Aires to our port of embarkation, Ushuaia passes off in a trance. I catch a cab to our cottage, which oversees the Martial mountain range. Trust Victoria to book something dramatic, even if just for a night. Her flight from Boston is delayed by a few hours.

I catch up on sleep, before incessant thumping awakes me. I peep through the half-ajar door. Spunky curls push through and envelope me in a tight embrace.

"Akhu, you've lost weight" – Victoria pinches my belly and dives onto the bed.

She could own any place, any crowd. Victoria Hussey was everything I yearned to be. 'The bindaas bitch from Boston' – as my university classmates used to address her.

"All set?" - I look at her solitary rucksack.

"Yeah, But you're most definitely not. Where's your other luggage?" – she stares at my 2 bursting-at-the-seams bags.

I chuckle. Victoria could stab me and I'd still giggle my way to the coffin.

Breeze whistles through the curtains. Shivering in my under-shirt, I move towards the window to latch it. A seagull swoons through loose puffs of vapor, finding the right air current to float on.

"Rose, the seagulls are moving south. I don't think we're far off from Terra Australis."

"Land!" –Pike shouts from the mast-head.

The crew shoots towards the hull with their spy glasses. But, what he took to be an island proves no more than a dark cloud lying low on the horizon. Land is a mirage in this desert of water.

A cackle erupts from the distance. A colony of Chinstrap penguins flap on an ice-float, about quarter of a mile in circuit. They must surely need to go onshore to breed.

"We must stay on course. Life doesn't throw an anchor everyday."

"And death is just around the corner, James."

"Rose, if we survive this storm, we'll take the world by storm." "A knighthood from the queen and…."

"And what about your family and….. your wife?"

I can't bear to look into her pale eyes anymore.

"James? Wow!"

I turn back and see Rose. No it's Victoria.

"Did you just call me James?"

"That's fascinating Fatso! Continue, continue." – she's sitting cross-legged, eyes and mouth wide open.

"No on-off switch here, dear!"

"How sad! Anyways, I'm going to crash for a bit. The ship departs in 5 hours."

There's a twinkle in her eyes as she moves to the adjoining room. She's holding a file with 'Confidential' printed on it.

*   *   *

The harbor is buzzing with activity and by afternoon, we're aboard the Plancius, an old Dutch naval vessel turned cruise-liner.

"Hi, my name is Robert Bronson and I'll be your shadow over the next 10 days." - our burly expedition leader welcomes us on the upper deck.

One by one, we introduce ourselves and I walk over to him for a quick handshake.

"Have we met before, Mr. Bronson?"

"Not sure, mate!"

"Mate? Mate! Bronson, call me mate again. I dare you…" – red-faced I move closer to him.

My hands are trembling and I don't back down despite the stale odor of meat and beer off his darned mouth.

Eyeball to eyeball we wage a silent war.

"We have to get back, captain. It's now or never." – Clerke butts in.

All the crew members look stunned, unable to react.

"I smell a mutiny. And that means death for a whole bunch of you lazy bastards."

"Captain, he's right." – Rose walks into the cabin.
She tugs on my shoulder pulling me back.

"Dramatics" – her nervous voice comes from behind.
"He's a bit….he loves to….uh never mind."

"Room 203, Akhu."

"What the….?"

"Yes, exactly. What the hell?!" Victoria pulls me aside.

"We need some rest." – she applies a medicinal patch
under her neck.

Wanting to experience sea sickness first hand, I decline
the help. The ship eases into open waters and will enter the
dreaded Drake's passage tomorrow.

I concentrate on the chart on our TV screen as Victoria
freshens up. The twin-sharing room is small, functional
and neat. We're cruising at 12 nautical miles an hour. Blank
swathes of water outside the porthole lull the ship and me
into a deep slumber.

I wake up in the middle of the night. Victoria's loud
snoring belies her petite frame. I put on my parka and
wobble up the upper deck.

The sun is lying low on the horizon. It's midnight. A
young crew member, Pedro walks up to me.

"How are you sir?"

"Did we just cross the Antarctic convergence? *71°
latitude!*"

"Wow, how did you….."

"Turn back"

"Sir – we've noticed a flock of penguins swim south-east.
Not too far off from land probably."

"NOW, you damned fool."

"Aye aye captain."

I pick up the map and scrawl the path furiously. 1773 will be the watershed year of my life. The journal shows 71° 40' S. The paper blots as tears roll down and mix with the ink. My ambition has to die today, but hopefully my love won't.

Rose won't survive if we don't turn back tonight. And so won't our baby. Darkness cloud up my eyes as the wooden walls converge on me and I lose consciousness.

"Akhu."

"Rose?" "No, you are not Rose." – I open my eyes to Victoria splashing water over my face.

"You alright?"

We settle down on a deck bench. Pedro leaves the two of us alone and resumes his duty. Cold wind burns my cheeks. I know we're not too far from land.

"Akhu, look at this. We've solved it."

She thwarts a chart in front of me. On top of the page is a line printed in bold.

'DNA 99.99% match. Cellular memory intact. James Cook vs Akhouri Byron Cook'

"I've been in touch with Dr. Dhingra over the past few months."

I look at her. Dazed. There's no anger at her for hiding this from me. Just numbness.

"You listening?"

I nod. A ray of light brightens the blue striations of the iceberg behind her.

"Your ancestral line meets that of the famed Mr. Cook. Your genetic code is aligned unbelievably close to the 18th century explorer. Your cells hold his memories."

My mind reels with myriad images. I can't distinguish fact from fiction. Rose from Victoria.

She gauges my discomfort and hands over another fax, probably received on the ship's communication center.

'To Victoria. Case no. 109. Confidential.'

The fax has an image of an old newspaper clipping.

'Rose Whitely, the daughter of the Mayor passed away aboard HMS Resolution amidst heated speculation that she and the Captain were having a clandestine affair. The reasons and timing of her death remain a mystery.'

Tears roll down my cheeks.

"If only I had turned the ship earlier…"

I lay my throbbing head on Victoria's shoulder.

"James Cook had no direct descendants. All his children either pre-deceased him or died without having children of their own. Or that's what the world believes….." "Except one, your great-great grandfather Ryan Cook, born to Rose onboard. She died in childbirth and Ryan was raised surreptitiously by one of James Cook's closest friends in Essex…."

"If only I had let go of my obsession…"

"Ryan Cook's only son and your great-grandfather later joined the East India company in Kolkata to never return…." "Mr. James Cook could never fulfil his ambition of discovering Terra Australis – which we now know as Antarctica. He died but his ambition did not……" "The latest research proves that in certain scenarios our cells carry residual memories, along with other genetic traits of our forefathers. And in your case his memories bloomed out through all the 5 senses."

"I should've turned back earlier…."

"Get a grip on yourself buddy! You are NOT James."

"But you are my Rose."

We hit the Antarctic Peninsula next morning. A 300 year old ambition finally sees fruition. I plug a rose into the snow.

'The universe is not required to be in perfect harmony with human ambition.'
- Carl Sagan

THE LEGEND OF YAM HA-MAVET

"As their skin and souls decay, your words should rise." – General Saladin

11th Century, Asia

"Aaaaaaaarkhh thoo" – Iblis spat out a broken tooth and dumped the leg piece behind crystallized rock salts.

The slurry of blood and flesh piled up high. Reminded him of Jebel Hafeet from back home. Just that this mountain wasn't baked with earth and stones. Bile retched up his throat and he threw up.

A low cloud cover drifted towards the lake, kissing her waif-like body. She floated on saline waters, shimmering due to the drowning sun.

"Beautiful sunset, eh?" – Aadam walked in from behind.

"How many left?"

"Two, but they're rotting."

He scrutinized the strapping kaafir. Aadam sounded earnest, but could he be trusted? They were the unlikeliest of allies thrown together in this netherworld. Whilst their armies resumed jihad someplace afar.

"Hmmm…."

He dismissed the conversation and got up. Energy had to be conserved. Also, befriending the boy would make the eventual task difficult.

"The water's turning choppy. Eve, come out now…" - Aadam's voice trailed, as Iblis dragged himself to the entrance of the cavern.

The stench of decaying flesh percolated the area. They had stacked the bodies inside another cave, a mile away. But now they'd have to burn off all that food.

He sat on the moist ground, arms wrapped around his knees. Cold limestone bit his skin at places where the sirwal was tattered. He pulled out the map from a crevice – graphed from their collective memories. They were probably two marhalas away from the nearest oasis.

He counted the inscriptions on the opposite wall. 27 days. The name 'Rashid' was carved out below yesterday's mark. His brother's death had been in vain. It was his fault. He should've sent Aadam to collect the fresh water. The quicksand would've sucked the kaafir's body then.

He scratched out a new mark and wrote 'Aadam' below it. It had to be done tonight. He tore off the cloth slung across his neck. He bit his lips, as pain shot through the dislocated shoulder. A month had passed since that glorious day.

"Hail Iblis" – shouted an enthusiastic soldier, plunging his sword into the heart of an already dead body.

Iblis gave the boy a rare smile and threw off his shield. He heard a crack in his left shoulder, but adrenalin mollified the pain. Beads of sweat dripped off his broad forehead. The wheat fields stank of death. Swords returned to their sheaths as the dust settled down. He raised his spear aloft.

"Hail Iblis" – a thousand voices boomed.

But his eyes wandered, searching for that one acknowledgement. And there he was, the great General Saladin, seated atop Rehmat, the finest Arabic horse ever. The General's finger pointed towards the village – the job was not yet over.

"Futuh…." – Iblis in turn, gestured towards the thatched huts.

Raucous laughter abound, as his men thundered off. To raze down the men and devour their women.

"Iblis" – a mellifluous voice broke his sleep.

"Yes, Ameera Evelyn?"

He noticed Evelyn's blistered skin below her ribs. She was now just a shadow of the full-bodied woman he'd met that day.

"Body's aching …" – she lay down on her belly.

"Where's that kaaf…. Aadam"

"Setting up the fire…Maybe. Anyway, who cares?"

He settled on her hips and massaged the back. As her muscles relaxed, he unbuttoned the hook and rested his naked torso on hers. The warm, clammy body acted like a soothing balm to his cold pains. Evelyn was so unlike her bawling sister.

The hut had a corpse lying at its entrance. He kicked the knight's body and slit off the head. As he broke through the door, two ladies huddled in front of a cot. The baby gurgled while he dangled its father's head in front of the cot.

"What's his name?"

The older woman clasped the cross, mumbling a prayer he hated so much.

"What is his NAME?" – he pressed the knife against her navel.

"Jos..joseph"- she retracted.

He blew air in his cupped fingers. Yes, the stench was unbearable for her. He glanced towards the younger girl. Fitful tears rolled down her ruddy cheeks.

"Ensure you name your son as Yusuf"

And in a moment of uncontrolled rage, he thrust his knife in the older woman's belly. Smoke and shrieks blustered up the chimney, as the younger one fell unconscious in his arms. He couldn't take his eyes off her face - angelic and pale against the darkness all around.

He joined the dancing soldiers outside. Pleasure of victory was somewhat marred by pain. The pain he saw on her face.

He bowed down to the general. The pock-marked face acknowledged with a curt nod. This was the fourth legion of knights, Iblis' regiment had hunted down.

"Thousands have sacrificed their lives for this day. They will travel to Jannat but…" – the general's voice rose. "Many kaafirs still live."

"Shall we burn down the village, general?"

Hundreds of villagers knelt besides the cadavers of their brethren. They awaited their destiny – quick swipe of a sword, scorching heat of fire or the slow thumping of stones.

"NO! Death is for the body. We should kill their souls."

The soldiers rounded youngsters from every household and shoved them before Iblis.

"You have served well, Captain Iblis. Now it's time for some rest."

The General then turned to the bards, scribbling on their papyrus.

"Ensure every day's degeneration is captured for posterity. As their skin and souls decay, your words should rise." "One day people will read your sonnets and never will any kaafir dare set foot on our holy land."

"Men, rejoice tonight for we march for our next jihad tomorrow." – Iblis left for his tent aware that this might be the last feast for a few of them.

The caravan trudged for days through shifting sands and gentle wadis, finally reaching an isolated lake. They left Iblis behind with a handful of men and the kaafirs, before moving on. General Saladin promised him a reunion after the holy month of Ramazan. But as mornings turned into nights and days into weeks, he realized no army was coming back. An ageing war veteran with a dislocated limb was unserviceable to the Ayyubids. They ruled Syria once again, but he wasn't a part of that glory.

5 of his men, 2 bards, his brother as well as 28 of the kaafirs had already perished. Yam ha-Mela, the sea of salt didn't discriminate against its victims. The war of Islam with Christianity withered away under this battle for survival.

"Have you re-created the map?" – Evelyn asked.

"Nearly there. We'll leave tomorrow. But we need water and meat for the journey." "It might be a fifteen day walk to civilization."

"So there are two…."

"Decayed" "Let's just do it tonight" – he whispered, puckering her earlobes

"Aadam loves me. No, I can't"

Darkness engulfed the last rays of a tired sun.

"But, WE HAVE TO SURVIVE"

"Maybe there are fish further down…"

He went silent. Both of them knew the truth. The water was too saline to hold any marine life, and they'd already stripped off all coconut trees.

He'd masterminded the hacking of every one of them. And now three of them remained. He had to leave this place at the earliest. His relationship with Evelyn had thawed over the last few weeks and he'd started dreaming a new life afar. But she still hadn't completely broken off ties with Aadam.

"Ok. Let's get him." – she whispered and her chapped lips rammed into his.

*　　*　　*

They gathered around the flames as Aadam roasted the final piece of meat, a salt-laced hand. Her cold fingers touched Iblis' back.

Evelyn broke into a couplet he hadn't heard before. Her voice touched a soulful note.

"Stars are guests of honour.....
and moonlight is the bride tonight.
Hold my hands.....
and walk the broken path."

He felt a queer knot building in his chest. He'd never felt so protective towards a woman, to any other human.

Now there was a dream, a hope. Hope of a normal life in the mountains far away. Hope of a life beyond survival, built with love and laughter. Evelyn was no longer a kaafir. Just the seed of a new life.

"I love you, Eve" – Aadam smiled and put a few more logs in the fire.

A raging dust-storm enveloped the moon in red hue. Iblis pricked his thumb, testing the jagged end of the knife.

"To love!" – he raised the coconut shell, drank the last drop and threw it in the fire.

He grabbed both of them in a tight hug, and closed his eyes. The chest relaxed - he felt peace. In the knowledge that he would be wielding a weapon, for the last time. A new life beckoned.

He visualized a brook flowing through the valley. A young toddler running out of a hut with a wooden sword, his hazel eyes smiling at them. 'Yusuf' – Evelyn's voice chiding the kid.

"To love" – she cried out.

This was the signal. Evelyn gave him a quick nod. Now was the moment.

"Aaah" – two voices cried out simultaneously.

Thick blood from Adam's back covered his wrists, as he thrust the knife into his backbone. But why was he feeling the pain? The other cry was his own. A sharp jab shot up his nape. He removed his free hand from Evelyn's waist and tried to touch his neck. A hand was in the way, pushing something deeper. His eyes rolled back as she smiled at him.

"I WILL SURVIVE" – Evelyn shouted and pushed the serrated stone further.

Life spurted out of him. He tumbled over the comatose body of Aadam. As he lay writhing uncontrollably, his eyes searched Evelyn's. For remorse, maybe a tear? Steely resolve stared back.

She pulled out the map from his sirwal and wrote the words 'Yam ha-Mavet', The Dead Sea with the X mark. She licked off the remaining blood and walked away, as darkness enveloped his eyes.

> *'The evil that men do lives after them;*
> *the good is oft interred with their bones.'*
> *– William Shakespeare*

THE KISS OF FAME

*"Every single one of us creates a pain point, as
the purpose to wade through life. Yours is divorce
and mine is...." ".....Love" – Deborah Gibson*

1991 North America

A kiss. That's all what she wanted. One simple kiss.

Not the dead peck they shared every night, but that full-throttled tangle of tongues. The melting of warm mouths, when everything else ceased to be. There was no body, no mind, no soul. Just the kiss. Lost, somewhere in pages of the past.

Debbie stubbed her cigarette on the magazine cover. It sizzled a hole through the image of a couple's lips. She rolled up the window, as the sun dissolved into concrete and fumes. The air was thick with smog. She popped a gum to drown the metallic taste of this city.

"Relax, Rog!" - the Bentley halted in front of a signal.

She dabbed on Vermilion lipstick. His favorite color. The strains of "I love you, California' hummed on the radio. Something was wrong with LA. The booming economy had softened its edges. Sleaze and violence no longer made headlines. Men were no longer men.

A billboard on the opposite street showcased her latest romcom, 'Love in Tokyo'. It garnered the biggest opening of the year, beating the mighty 'Terminator 2'. Debbie vs Arnie was an unlikely battle at the box-office. Personally, she preferred neither of these genres. Indie cinema was her thing but producers weren't backing pathos, anymore. Audiences preferred glossy fluffiness over brutal realities of life. LA was turning into a sissy.

As they approached the boulevard, she could sense a buzz. The cacophony of neon lights dulled the night sky. They slowed down, halting some distance before the handrails.

"Slightly ahead."

"Hmmm.." – Roger grunted.

She noticed his bloodshot eyes in the rear-view mirror. "All ok with Stefanie?"

"I can't stand her anymore! Divorce is the only option."

"Why? Just because she won't strip to pay for your lifestyle."

"But the money is good there"

"Then why the heck did you pull her out, in the first place?!"

"Well, it's easy for a million dollar baby to pass judgment."

"Let's not kid ourselves. This has nothing to do with money. You're just plain bored."

She ignored the jibe. Apart from being her chauffer-agent-bodyguard, Roger was also a great friend. But so was Stefanie.

"Blah blah…" - Roger wagged his fingers.

"Every single one of us creates a pain point, as the purpose to wade through life. Yours is divorce and mine is…." "…..Love"

The word came out in a hushed tone. It weighed heavy on her tongue. It was almost bastardized in today's world.

Roger shifted uneasily in his seat. She sensed his embarrassment for being rude earlier. She flicked on aviators to hide her puffy eyes, as a valet opened the door.

At the entrance of Kodak theatre, tuxedos and evening gowns jostled to get one glimpse of her. Hollywood Boulevard was on steroids tonight. She adjusted her gown to reveal the assets that had given her entry into stardom. These were remnants of a life gone by. Of a life when she was the queen of another world. He'd pulled her out of a dungeon and eased her into this heady concoction of money, drugs and fame.

The flashbulbs went into overdrive, as she stepped out. Goosebumps swamped her bare skin. She put on her famous Friday evening pout and waved to the mob. A Michael Jackson look-alike moonwalked towards her with a rose. Roger stalled the impostor in his tracks.

She knelt down besides the 2500th star, freshly embedded on the tarmac. The five-pointed terrazzo and brass star read 'Deborah Gibson'.

You'll be the sun amongst stars here! – the memory of his voice gushed in.

She replayed the line in her mind. The words weren't important. The voice was. Ten years back they'd walked as nobodies, on this very street.

"Congrats Debbie!" – fans raised her photo cut-outs.

"How do you feel to be inducted into the hall of fame?" – an eager rookie from TMZ jumped out in front of other paparazzi.

Everyone wanted a sound bite from Hollywood's favorite controversy child. It had been one hell of a journey. From shambles to shame to fame. Three distinct lives in one single lifetime.

"Feel a bit old, now that this piece of metal has been engraved... Should've got it much earlier though." – her fingers ran through the pixie cut.

The hair, the bosom, the pout – all part of a plan. Devised by him, executed by her. To create the perfect diva.

"Not a single Academy award ever. Not even a nomination! Do you think you still deserve this?" – an old, cratered face pointed to the star below.

"LA needs a dream, not pseudo-intellectualism served by your Oscar types. And Debbie is that dream which makes you wet every night!" – she winked at the reporter.

"And how's the celebration…." – another voice trailed as she wandered to the side.

She started Lindy Hopping with a couple of girls, decked up in garish outfits. Sanity was found in these silly moments, apart from being in his arms. She was going to quit all this tonight. To spend every moment with him, tomorrow and forever. He won't reciprocate her feelings. But she knew he still loved her.

Their bond couldn't be ravaged by time or circumstances. He'd rescued her from the depravity of Vegas, 12 years back. The mark didn't allow her to forget those days. She'd slashed her wrist then to seek freedom, only to find herself in his arms.

After quitting the strip-club, she acted in her first film under his direction. 'The Kiss' got panned by critics as nothing but a soft-porn docudrama. But they moved on. It was a small role in 'The Godfather', which finally got her noticed. And slowly, the sea of Hollywood engulfed her.

The crowd was getting restless. Roger closed in with the guards to form a barrier.

"Last question, please" – he shouted over the din.

"You do only love stories. But we heard Aasim…."

Aasim. So the name hadn't withered away. Not yet. She didn't hear the remainder.

"Bye" – she gestured Roger towards the car.

She'd contemplated quitting a long time back. But Aasim wouldn't have wanted her to. Not before this day.

But today it was – the very last day. The loneliness of love is infinitely better than the loneliness of stardom. No chocolate-dipped, creamy strawberry movies anymore. Their ambition was fulfilled. They could now spend rest of their lives, away from the poisoned saccharine of arc lights.

It was past midnight as they drove back. She pinched herself and dilated her pupils. She was an insomniac by choice and slept in fits and naps. Going into depths of the subconscious was scary. What if she never woke up or worse, woke up not able to move.

Roger slowed down in front of the glass mansion at Beverly hills junction.

"Debbie, we have a shoot tomorrow afternoon."

"Cancel all appointments till I call you."

"You sure? Everything alright?"

"Bye."

She entered the sprawling bedroom. Curtains fluttered in front of the open balcony. There were no windows. No walls. Only glass all around. Just the way Aasim liked the house to be. Open and bright.

Tulips ordered from Amsterdam were neatly arranged on the side table. She'd asked Mary to take the day off.

Aasim's snoring permeated the room. She put their favorite Charlie Chaplin movie in the player and pulled out a can from the cabinet.

"Pepsi? Or you still on your dietary marathon?" - she moved across the bed towards him.

They hadn't touched weed or alcohol since that day. He stirred, as she pressed her body against his.

"Should I give you a shave, dear?" – the week-old stubble tickled her.

She took a gulp and threw the can in the bin.

"Happy Anniversary, A."

She kissed him tenderly. As every other night, his lips did not react. Aasim opened his eyes, the paralyzed body unable to move or smile. But she knew his heart was still beating - happy and sad. Today was their marriage anniversary.

Ten years back, post their vows they drank and doped through the evening. And in a mad rush late night, she'd crashed their car on Hollywood Boulevard. And since that day, the kiss was lost. Lost, somewhere in the pages of the past.

> *'Love is not breathlessness, it is not excitement, it is not the desire to mate every second of the day. It is not lying awake at night imagining that he is kissing every part of your body.*
>
> *No... don't blush. I am telling you some truths. For that is just being in love; which any of us can convince ourselves we are.*
>
> *Love itself is what is left over, when being in love has burned away' – A quote from* **Captain Corelli's Mandolin**

Alpha Nyani's Tryst with Destiny

"Wraaaoooookhoo…" – Alpha Nyani

2 Million BC, Africa

Lava gurgled in the pit of mother mountain, many forests away. Alpha Nyani eyed a ray of light peeping through the canopy of Baobabs. If it was a full moon night, it might be his last. But he didn't want to die. Not yet.

"Wraaaoooookhoo" – he tried producing that high-pitched sound. Not perfect, probably not loud enough.

Flapping his ears, he lumbered around the spot. The gash on his bony forehead attracted a galaxy of flies. Clenching his jaw, he pulled again. But the branches wouldn't break. They further scraped his skin, searing the hair on his wrists.

A ruffle atop the adjoining tree distracted Alpha. Naked heads sunk in hunched feathers, awaited his death. A twig changed colors and opened its eyes. He snapped but his tongue barely kissed its tail, as the chameleon sprung away. He masticated on his own saliva to kill hunger. As the rising moon lit the plains, a boogle of weasels scurried into their burrows. They kept away from the baobabs, ignorant that their predator was tied. Helpless. Alone.

Alpha gazed at the twinkling objects above. Every night, the sky painted beasts, otherwise found deep in the jungle. Tonight he could see the outline of a bear. The one animal he'd been aping since childhood. And whose posturing he'd now perfected.

Alpha wriggled up on his hind legs like the grizzly, to purview any dangers ahead. This was the third successive summer, they had to abandon home in search of new woodlands. The colossal lizards had vanished. Forest fires raged through the continent and rains were a distant memory. Mother mountain that first erupted when he was an infant was bubbling again. Their land was mutating.

The Nyanis had the knack for recognizing patterns, an instinct not found in any of their cousins. Neither the bonobos nor the gorillas. Following the death of his father, he was anointed Alpha. And he had to lead them at a time, when their existence itself was in danger. They waddled through grasslands in the direction from where the ball of fire rose every morning.

Under cloudless skies, the balding bodies smoldered as they trudged along on their knuckles. They hadn't had any kill for the past week. Alpha clutched a handful of grass and masticated. He grinned, as others spat out shreds, trying to mimic his action. His eyes locked on a dark haired female lagging behind the clan. A bit lost. She scratched her fingernails into the mud, glancing at him every other second. She was young with no mate, no baby. Beta1 nudged her and started scratching her back. But her eyes were fixed on Alpha, the virile leader. He sprung towards them and squared up in front of Beta1.

"Khoo khoo khoo" – the opponent's eyes scrutinized him.

Nostrils flared, Alpha took half a step forward and walloped the protruding jaw of Beta1. A grunt, a snivel and Beta1 folded down between Beta2 and Beta3. He had the first right. How dare they stand up to him.

The group of five were getting bolder by the day. They despised the unilateral power that Alpha held. He'd gauged their desire for a new structure. One which would have a cluster of leaders, instead of him alone.

Suddenly there was a commotion in the bush behind. Alpha sniffed but the smells were mixed up. Fear and hope in equal measures. A familiar chatter grated his ears. The dried wounds burnt his chest, as it swelled in anticipation.

"Grrr…" – a pair of nails dug into his back.

His blood licked the cold air. Beta1 breathed down his neck as the others wobbled towards him.

"Khoo khoo" – Beta3 and Beta4 moved in closer.

Narrowing his glassy eyes, he groaned and shook his mane.

"KHOO KHOO" – his gargantuan frame loomed over them, canines ready to bite into their flesh.

They retracted a step, fear for their old leader still seeping through.

"Ooorf Ooorf Ooorf…" – the baobabs shook violently, as baboons swung in from all directions.

So the Betas had inducted these fiery-tailed idiots into their coterie. A thunderous clap resounded in the air. Everyone peered at the sky. Another streak of lightning tore through the dark clouds. As soon as they part and the moon sets, his heart would be torn out from the body.

The baboons threw their collectibles in a heap and squatted around it. The Betas broke through the circle and devoured the mish-mash of insects, fruits and flesh of a dead wildebeest. The remainder of Nyani clan was missing. Probably slaughtered. Amidst the chatter, Alpha heard a faint howl of someone galloping in the distance.

"Wraoookhoo…" – he called out.

Was it them?

The Nyanis continued their march eastwards. He could taste salt in the air, as a sloshing sound ebbed and rose ahead. They were approaching a mammoth water body.

A soft cry stemmed from the shrubs to his left. He hurried towards the source. Two hyenas circled a wolf baby, drool dripping down their loathsome faces. Alpha glanced around for any sign of the pup's parents. Why was this baby alone?

Beta5 caught up with Alpha and nudged him towards their marching direction. This was not their fight. Also, it was not an ape baby. Why should they bother? He knew they had to move on - four clan members had starved to death. Most of them hadn't yet developed the appetite for grass. Beta5 ambulated away from the distraction. Shoulders slouched, Alpha followed.

But, was it right to leave? How then were the Nyanis different from others? As an Alpha, what example was he setting?

The forests were dying. The big cats won't be able to rule much longer. This was the right time. If he wanted to lead the Nyanis to glory, he had to think beyond the apes. Mother Earth needed a new species to take over. And they could provide her with the answer.

Some distance ahead, he noticed his mate playing with their child in a patch of muddy water. Whilst his own baby was nestled in the safety of the clan, the wolf pup was left behind to be slaughtered. His child looked up and their eyes met for a split second.

He rammed back in the opposite direction, and sprang in front of the hyena. The pup was hanging from its fangs.

"khi khi khi" – the second hyena crept up behind Alpha.

"Khoo khoo"

"khi khi khi"

"KHOO KHOO" - he thumped his chest, towering over the hyena in front.

Tail bristled, it dropped the baby and whimpered away with its partner. Alpha sat down and cradled the pup in his arms. The infant stopped wailing, as he stroked the fur around its face.

"wraoo…" - the infant snuggled close to his chest.

It wagged its tail and licked his face till it almost tickled him.

"Wraaoooooooo" – Dust flew all around, as a pack of wolves galloped towards the clearing.

He placed the baby on a dry patch, readying himself for battle. The largest wolf halted in front of him, its amber eyes locked into his own. Ruffs of grey hair framed its face, and the pointed muzzle smelt him inquisitively. Without exchanging a sound, Alpha got down to his fours and touched its forehead. A silent bond was forged that day.

Alpha nudged the infant towards its parents and loped off to catch up with his clan. They wouldn't have seen the baby as innocent or harmless. They would've seen it as a burden or even a threat to their safety from the wolf pack.

As Alpha reached closer, he heard a loud cry. He pushed his way through the group jostled around someone. His eyes fell on the bloodied infant tucked in his dead mate's arms. Beta1 wiped off blood from his face, as the group of five moved away from the two dead bodies. The rest of the clan froze, startled into inaction by the ghastly sight. Alpha's vision clouded. Images from the past floated in his mind.

The day when their baby was born. A bundle of blood, bones and hair, as his tired mate opened her eyes.

The first toothy grimace when it ate mud. The cold nights when it nuzzled on his belly, fingers curled around his thumb. The first time it learnt to swing, hanging on to their arms.

Even images of what had not yet happened. The baby growing up to be Alpha one day. He and his mate watching the *ball of fire go down the ocean, as the new Alpha led this world. But reality leached in to the dream.*

The day when their baby was unborn. A bundle of blood, bones and hair, as his tired mate closed her eyes.

Alpha wiped tears off his eyes and charged towards Beta1, nailing him to the ground. He started pounding his face, wanting to smash it into a pulp. As soon as he picked up a stone from the side, his arms stuck in the air. He roared and flayed his body around, as two Betas on each side struggled to hold on. They pinned him down and pulverized his torso. The old loyalists from the clan jumped into the fray to save him. A massive fight ensued, as darkness enveloped his bloodied eyes. When he woke up, he found himself tied to a tree in this sparse woodland. To be slaughtered in the traditional Nyani way, towards the end of the full moon night. And a new Alpha would be anointed.

A gust of wind chilled his tired bones, as the night progressed. The primates lazed in a circle with a couple of Betas scratching stones, trying to start a fire.

He heard it again. Was it them? His nostrils twitched as a lupine scent floated in from the east. The putrid smell was sweet tonight. It reeked off revenge.

"Wraaaoooooookhoo…" – he strained through every ounce of air in his lungs.

"Khoo khooo" – the Betas bared their teeth.

They started hooting and mocking him. They'd always despised Alpha's habit of making strange noises. Of trying to connect with other beasts.

Beta1 raised his hand to silence the group. He pointed eastwards. A sneer crossed Alpha's face, as he heard the echo. The savannah resounded with paws galloping in.

"Wraaooo….Wraaooo…." – the howl grew louder, as they neared the bush.

"Wraoo….wraoooo…" - ten wolves dashed in, halting around Alpha.

They formed a wall between him and the primates. The largest grey wolf walked towards him. They locked their foreheads.

Sharp teeth gnawed through the branches tying him down. Alpha shrugged his shoulders to shake off the last strands. He plucked off a scrambling squirrel and chomped ravenously, eyes following every single movement of the Betas.

Strangely enough, the primates started disbanding. The ensuing chaos confounded the wolves, and their feet fidgeted unsure whom to focus on. Beta1 clambered over a rock and gestured towards the other four. Each Beta collected two baboons and sprang in different directions. That's when Alpha realized their plan. He knew the wolves wouldn't stand a chance if these trios marked each individual and launched from a height. The primates encircled the isolated wolves, grunting angry noises.

Beta1 let out a cry and raised his arms in the air. In a flash, the primates mounted a ferocious attack. Wild scratching ensued as the wolves fought off the nails, trying to bite off whatever came their way. They kept switching directions in a mad rush to avoid the pounding. The primates were exploiting their newfound ability to stand on two.

In a corner, the youngest wolf made a sudden leap and snapped off Beta2's head. The baboons attached to Beta2 loped away as they lost their leader. But Beta1 growled from his perch, pointing them towards a group where another wolf tore open the chest of a baboon. They jumped atop the wolf and gouged out its eyes.

Alpha moved away from the action and concentrated on Beta1 who was orchestrating the primates. He was filling up gaps. When a primate died, he sent re-enforcements from wherever the baboons had already butchered a wolf. Many years back, Alpha's clan defeated a pride of cats using this strategy. Beta1 had learnt well.

Alpha marched over to the wildebeest carcass and pulled off a sharp bone. He dragged it towards the big, grey wolf. He sat on the wolf, constricted his lips and blew out air. At this signal, the wolf started trotting towards Beta1. A baboon leapt at them but Alpha ducked the strike. Balancing himself, he held the bone firmly as the wolf soared over the rock. With one swift move he struck the shrapnel through Beta1's throat and twisted. A shriek pierced through the woods as Beta1's body quivered to the ground in a heap. Alpha threw the bone aside and thundered, beating his chest wildly.

Everyone froze at the sight of blood oozing out of Beta1's dislocated head. The wolves quickly blocked off the retreating Betas.

Alpha gathered dried leaves as the primates huddled together. He rubbed two stones and set a twig on fire. The flame ignited the adjoining dry bush and started spreading to the entire area. He pulled out a young female baboon atop his wolf and the pack rode off towards the sea. The remainder primates chattered and tried to scamper, but there was no exit route as the flames blew high.

"Wraookhoo" – he pointed to the narrow strip of land, stretching over the mass of water around.

He turned around to see the burning forest. The screams filled his heart with peace. And that day, Alpha Nyani became the first man and the wolf his pet dog. They rode out of Africa in search of greener pastures, inventing language in the bargain.

> *'It is not the strongest of the species that survives, nor the most intelligent.*
> *It is the one that is most adaptable to change.'*
> **– Charles Darwin**

SMERT

"What a great feeling must that be! Living in the moment...." "I feel lost every moment, as I keep planning for my next." – David Whitaker

1960 – South America

He shreds the photograph and flushes its fragments. Bye, bye Lindsay.

There's a knock on the bathroom door. As gentle as the fingers behind it.

"Coming" – he adjusts his bow in the mirror.

Twirling his moustache, he sucks in the belly. Despite spending half his life on flights and hotels, he's managed to hold on. He admires his faded leather jacket. Shaves five years off him. Silmara thinks he's not a day above forty. 'Rich, powerful and single!' A lie hidden somewhere in it. Like most other maxims of life.

But the veil won't last longer. How to break the news to these two headstrong women of each other's existence is a challenge. The old hag might be easier compared to the new life.

He eases into the living area of the suite. She's relaxing on the futon, stilettos flung across the rug. A dense mole sits pretty on her thigh.

"I'm só hungrrry" – Silmara rolls her eyes as if about to faint.

The hearth flames flicker. Her sequin dress plays a game of light and shadows, teasing him.

"Two chicken fajitas and another bottle of Chardonnay. And make it quick."

He checks the phone wires for presence of any tapping device. Silmara raises her eyebrow in a mock arch of suspicion.

Rain trickles down the French window facade. The suite seems presidential against the line-up of favelas, outside. Naked children run across drenched streets.

"2 years. Chéérrs!"

"Yes, who can forget that ethereal evening that changed my life…"

"Ouurrr lives" – she raises her glass.

"Beautiful Mozart symphony. This is life!" – he broke into the circle.

The European delegates were in full force during the peace conference. Rumors of a potential third world war had to be quenched.

"Not bad, Mr. Whitaker! You know your music." – the French President smiled.

France's successful nuclear test in the Sahara had added an edge to his girlish voice.

The violin notes hit a crescendo, as the group sipped their wines. It was good to break the political debate raging in the afternoon with a relaxed evening. Only the Soviets had stormed out in the afternoon. Nikita Khrushchev was conspicuous by his absence, throughout.

"Bééthooven, sirrr"

"Excuse me?"

"Sorry, may I pour you ánother rround?"

The server had a polite air of confidence. Hair tied in a neat bun, she oozed Latin elegance. Her Spanish sounded different. Mexican maybe. The tan seemed recently acquired, though.

"No Thanks….By the way, why do you say Beethooven – that's Mozart!"

"*Lúdwig ván Bééthooven, Mozarrt's junior by fiftéén yearrs, was deeply influenced by his work.*" "*Maybe that's why many mistake his cádenzas to Mozart's D minor piano concerto*"

"*What's your name?*"

"*What's in á name?*" – *she smiled and sashayed with her tray to the next set of guests.*

"*Just excuse me for a minute, gentlemen.*" – *he moved away from the delegates.*

He paused for her to finish serving the next group, and tapped on her shoulder.

"*Another glass possible?*"

"*Oh…Ofcourrrrse sirr, which one?*"

"*You decide, Ms. 'What's in a name'*"

"*A mán of yourrr class should go for DRC.*"

"*DRC?*"

"*Domáine Romanée-Conti.*" "*From the turrrn of the centurry. Vintáge 1899*"

Fine taste for a waitress! Though she looked more like a diva.

She poured the sparkling wine and their fingers brushed, as the glass stem slipped through her hand and burgundy splashed onto the tuxedo.

"*I'm só só sorrrry*" – *she started stroking his shirt.*

"*Is there a place I can dry myself? Away from the prying eyes of these pretentious people.*"

She led him to a secluded room on the floor below. The door closed behind them. It was damp and dark. Her breathing grew heavy as she closed in with a towel.

His arms brushed her bosom and he could sense a yes written all over her. Body language was his mother tongue and he knew that every cell of hers yearned for him.

And today too, he senses a big yes written all over her.

"So will you shift to DC with me?"

"Will you ásk?"

"Ofcourse, I love you!" – the words sound hollow. Wooden.

Lust, most definitely. Love, he isn't sure.

"Liar, liarrr" – she plugs in the LP.

The scratchy pre-amble matches the rhythmic cackle of the burning wood. He re-fills their glasses.

"To á new lurrve. To us."

"To us."

"You've got all that á man would everrr want" – she strokes the \scar on his face. "But steeel this restlessness?"

There's a knock. He opens the door and aroma of fresh guacamole fills the room. As the waitress lays the table, he observes the way she holds the towel in her right hand.

Silmara leads him towards the window, her slender reflection dignifying the ghetto outside. Rio hasn't changed a bit, from the time he first came here.

The waitress exits the room. Why did she leave the food on the side table instead of the dining area? No thank you. No good bye. Why the hurry? Poor training. He makes a mental note to complain later.

He strokes Silmara's hair as guitar strains jive with samba drums.

"Who's the artist?"

"Joé Sextext" – she sways to the latino rhythm.

He clicks his fingers and starts tap dancing. Silmara never ceases to amaze him. Despite a probable rise from poverty, she's acquired an exhaustive range of interests - from music to architecture, and sometimes the esoteric world of political science too. An ideal companion for the life ahead.

"You still háven't answerrred my question!"

"Which one, sweetheart?"

"Why thees restlessness?"

"Are you really happy?"

"What is it with you Amerrricáns? Question for a question – but neverrrr án answer!"

"Alright alright" – he raises his hands.

He loses his balance and tumbles on the floor. The drinking has to stop – they aren't allowed to lose control. But then who cares. This is the night when he reloads life. He fiddles with the diamond ring in his jacket.

"I'm going to be appointed the Defense Secretary of…"

"The Unitéd States of Amerrrrica!" – she completes with a chuckle.

Silmara lifts his arms aloft and whistles.

"But I'm not sure if that's what I yearn for."

He rotates his shoulders in slow, circular moments. The pain returns. This life of duplicity comes with a million dollar stress tag. Heartburns, Spinal pain, the incessant nagging of conscience. Every day blurs the demarcation between truth and deceit. The woman in front, doesn't know she's dating a married man. Fidel Castro whom he met last week, isn't aware of the Bay of Pigs operation. And Lindsay would be shocked when the divorce papers reach her.

He wants to turn back time. Come face to face with his 15-year old self and slap him. On the day when he stole the quiz papers in Pennsylvania and topped his class. That's when the downward spiral of the soul began.

Silmara yanks him closer and guides his palms to the contour of her hips. His eyes follow the veins swimming down her neck. Her waist seems strange today, ungainly.

"The weight of living up to an image, lying to the world has made me lose my real identity. Truth is a concept, which I don't understand anymore."

"Truth Senorrrr?? What is truth if not creative imagination of the rich and the powerrrful?"

"Hmmm…..Now your turn to answer – are you happy?"

"Si right now, because I'm in your arrrms…." "And it doesn't matter what happened beforrre or what is going to happen next."

He squeezes her closer. They are wide awake - to the proximity, to the mingling of their warm breaths.

"How great a feeling must that be. Living in the moment…." "I feel lost every moment, as I keep planning for my next."

"I was lost too, but meeting a man with a higherrr purpose has revived me"

"Higher purpose?"

"Serrrrving your country! Saving it?"

She folds in his arms, tresses dropping over his shoulder.

His heart thumps as she leads him towards the bed. She unbuttons his shirt to reveal white tufts of hair. But he's no longer conscious; the inebriated state helps.

"What is it that's weighing on yourrrr mind..." "I can be, how do you say? Ummm… an agony aunt"

The music has stopped and the fire dies down. The night is beautiful. Silent. He cups his mouth - the throat is dry, choked.

"Their missile system might not be a deterrent for our Turkish placements." "The Russians will use Cuba to start off a nuclear war. The Cold war is heating up to a destructive conclusion….And we…"

She moves in closer resting her head on his bare chest. "We what?"

"We plan to ambush and bombard…So many innocent Cubans. This burden, how will I live with it?"

"Al vivo todo le falta, y a l muerto todo le sobra" – she interrupts

His Spanish is rudimentary but he's heard this saying before. *For one who's alive nothing's quite enough, while for one who's dead anything's too much.*

"What?"

"You won't have to face that burden."

He can just see the outline of her face as she switches off the light. Her sweaty body presses against his. A metallic strap protrudes over her gut.

"Death, deceit, life, truth…Meaningless words all theez."

His mind is spinning. Nothing is coherent – his thoughts, her words. She pulls out a small microphone from under her bra and throws it aside. He stretches for the gun under the pillow. But it's missing and so is the classified file.

"That bloody waitress…."

"Yezzz, my love" – her Mexican Spanish accent morphs to Russian

"Who are…"

She seals a tape on his mouth.

"Hope you forgive me. We will mee..but not as adverzaries….."

The words sound garbled.

"Nastya Koronav….KGB….Following you….2 yearz"

He can barely make out the words.

Who are you? – his eyes question her again.

"Smert" "That eez the only truth of life. We are getting freedom. From my sorrow and your restlessness"

He tries to wriggle off the bed, but neck down, his limbs don't move.

"The wine eez different. Must complain, no?" "Russia, Cuba….never allow US, Turkey…no world war."

He eyes the strap as she sits on his thigh. The ticking of the belt goes up a notch.

"Someday, I will meet you in the fieldz of Siberia. Hope you come." – she whispers and hugs him.

He strangely feels light. A burden lifted off his soul. A life of deceit couldn't have got a better ending. He prays for Lindsay's good life ahead. He looks at Silmara, Nastya, Smert. Smert he remembers means death in Russian. The beautiful death hugs him one last time.

The ticking noise reaches a crescendo. She removes the tape. Her lips touch his. And there's a loud explosion – the sulphur chokes him for a split second and then nothingness. Darkness, bliss, Smert.

> *'In times of universal deceit, telling the truth*
> *is a revolutionary act.'*
> *– George Orwell*

ALEKS IN WONDERLAND

"So here I am, a foolish love-stricken woman
who is now nothing but a whore - with clientele
ranging from the would-be pope to men similar to
the ones, who raped you thirty years back." – Elena

15th Century, Europe

"…And whoremongers, and sorcerers, and all liars shall have their part in the lake which burneth in fire and brimstone.….Which is the second death."

He closed the gilded Bible and paused. The congregation filled the room with hushed whispers. So far it was going exactly as per sequence.

"Rise o people of this city. Clean up the filth which is clogging the soul of Amsterdam" – his voice boomed over the pulpit.

A pigeon fluttered across the hall and nestled in a fissure on the ceiling. He made a mental note to whip Rudolph later. The Oude Kerk roof was now the highest in Europe. Such imperfections were not tolerable. But this old church was just a stepping stone. Tonight they would swap the final dream. His skeletal fingers traced the red letters.

The pope will rise and clap first, followed by others. And you better get your dick moving towards our nest, my reverend Aleksander.

A smile crept on his blackened lips and he tore off the papyrus, ears tuned to the silent hall. A clap echoed from the centre, and like a ripple, within minutes the entire hall was applauding.

It was a good turnout. And a great turnaround too, considering the shambles earlier. The mob had vandalized most of the church fittings over the years. Except for paintings on the high ceiling. Until a decade back, the locals used to gather here just to gossip. Peddlers and thieves sold their wares and beggars sought shelter.

He, Aleksander de Boer was instrumental in cleaning up the mess. He'd overlooked the physical as well as social revamp. So what, if the homeless were expelled. Sacrifice is always a precursor for progress.

But this world seemed puny now. His greatness had to reach beyond these four walls. Real power lay in Rome. Whilst the French and Italian factions fought, a Dutchman would whisk away the crown now. The Roman Catholic Church was his final destination, the holy grail. He beckoned Rudolph to escort the pope. The old man gingerly ascended the stairs and touched Alek's shoulders, before beginning his speech. He driveled about the importance of the church in today's debased world.

Every word was set – he'd handwritten them during the last Dream Swap with Elena. He scratched the dirt on the lectern, counting the final words. She was waiting. Tonight would be special.

The pope fumbled with his closing note. Few youngsters exited from the back door. The Roman Catholic Church needed someone more dynamic than a bumbling, half-deaf geriatric. They needed him, the world's next messiah.

"Bishop De Boer, the Vatican is proud of what you're doing for this town."

"Trying to emulate you, your Holiness" - he held the pope's hand and bowed.

"The college of pontiffs needs you..." – the words were hushed but he knew them verbatim. "See me in Italy next month."

Warm blood rushed through his body, and he felt himself tower over every other person in the room.

"Aye" - he led the old man down the stairs and across the aisle.

Everyone bowed as the pope's entourage strode towards the main door.

"By the way, you need to change these" – the pope pointed to the floor.

It consisted of gravestones, as the church was originally built on a cemetery. Alek's nostrils flared, as he nodded. Nobody could order him. Not in his own backyard. Not anywhere. Not anymore.

The crowd trickled out, leaving him and Rudolph behind.

"You managed the sermon well, sire"

"Hmm" – his shadow loomed over the wall.

Moonlight poured through the stained glass and the cathedral basked in kaleidoscopic hues.

"Blow off the candles." - he limped towards the back door.

"Bishop, may I accompany you?"

"Nee"

"Please bishop sire, I…"

"NO. Go and get some rest, Rudolf"

The plaintiff had outlived his usefulness. Time was ripe to flog his vitals and dispense him from service.

With the bowler hat pulled down his forehead, Aleks was unrecognizable. He could pass off as one of the growing tribe of Dutch traders ruling the seven seas. He put on a tweed jacket and opened the door. A blast of cold air smashed his cheeks.

'Excellent weather.' - he thought as his fingers juddered.

Not many would venture out on a frigid autumn evening. As he ambled towards De Wallen, the silence of the night grew heavy. The nothingness had an incessant sound. It was the crickets. The males chirped away, trying to attract females. He sneered. This phase was over for him. Elena was already under control.

He glanced behind every minute, almost expecting the boys to creep up. It had been four decades, since that night. But he could still hear the child's screams. His screams. Aleksander de Boer was powerless then. Just a poor farm kid who didn't even know what rape meant. The mental scars never healed and neither did the limp.

Many years later, he picked up an orphan from that very street. Rudolph was a stand-in for those unknown boys who'd raped him. Surrogate revenge was like beer. Bitter and disgusting but able to drain out the pain, nonetheless. Gulp by gulp. Ache by ache.

Maple leaves dotted the canal edge. A calm Amstel reflected the full moon - ideal for their Dream Swap. A dinghy drifted by, and he pulled up the muffler to hide his scarred, hollow cheeks.

Rats scurried through trash piles, littered around the bridge corner. He spat and strolled down a narrow lane. Smoke emanated from shops and raucous laughter filled this part of the town. He pulled out dry weed from his pocket and rolled it into a cigar. Publicly, he'd denounced it as the banc of Amsterdam. But then like every vice it was heavenly indeed.

He leaned onto a wall and smoked out rings, eyes fixed on a dilapidated house. He was about to roll his third cigar, when light shone behind the red curtains.

"What in the name of Satan!" – he muttered as a couple of other houses in the row were also shining now. Bright and red.

Face down, he hobbled to the last cottage and pulled the bell rope. His heart raced, as her voluptuous silhouette moved behind the curtains. There were pleasures to be had, but he didn't want to lose focus. He replayed the sequence of events he had to dream tonight.

The door opened and cheap, lavender scent filled his lungs. He strained his eyes to surf through the room illuminated by dying candles.

Her shadow danced on the bedroom wall, waiting. The wooden floor creaked as he crouched through the passage.

"Elena!!!" – he wigwagged at the fluttering curtains.

She closed the window. He couldn't take any chances now. Not when he was so close. Tonight was the final phase of the perfect plan. The final Dream Swap. Nay, one dream and the other a nightmare. To be swapped for the perfect ending.

"Aleks...." – the whisper lingered as she moved in closer.

He noticed the dark mark on her nape. Not many parts of the body were left bare. Though, he needed just one. He scrutinized the cramped room. This was the last time. On the side table was a black & white photo of baby Elena with her grandma. The cleft on the chin was the only feature seemingly common, between the innocent toddler and the amorous woman in front of him.

The room was strewn with tattered mosquito nets, plastic ashtrays, bawdy mannequins and weird wigs. Paintings and graffiti cluttered the opposite wall. A sign of the many artists having passed through. He'd dreamt of sleeping with different partners during one of their Dream Swaps, effectively rendering her a prostitute. This way, the angle of love had been crossed off.

As a side-effect, the entire street had been sullied. Candle lit cottages with rouge curtains invited ravenous visitors. De Wallen was now called the red light area, a euphemism for the whore houses these cottages had become. He'd ensured decay of this city, this country. A decadence which he'd eventually be called upon to clean up one day.

Her calloused hands removed his coat.

"It worked, the pope has…."

"Shhh"

"Is this always necessary?" – he removed the bottle from her hand.

He tore off her flimsy robe and puckered her nipples. Slow and strong. Sunrise was many hours away.

"Sire…….." "I'm returning to Albania, next week."

"But the dream…"

"Is that it?" – she pushed him aside and leaned against the ledge. "What about the love you professed?"

"Love? Love!" "Purity and debauchery, the twain shall never…" – he bit his tongue as soon as the words came out. "Come here, sweetheart"

'Easy' he whispered to himself. There was still one dream to be swapped tonight.

He looked into her eyes – for all the filth she was, her gaze always unnerved him. It had a sense of purity contrasteren to her surroundings. Beyond the much abused body lay a clean soul.

He kissed her to stall further conversation. He couldn't renounce his dream. Not for her, not now when he was so close to fulfilling it. Anyways, she was too raggedy for a future together. The penurious make-up, sex with strangers and insomnia had taken its toll.

He pursed her lips open and emptied the bottle. The intoxication would numb her pain. But the swap had to be done while she was still in her senses.

"Mami" – she cried as he poured molten wax on her right thigh.

He gnashed his teeth as burning wax scathed his left thigh, as well. They huddled together like a pair of conjoined twins - his cold body against her warmth.

"Mmmmzzzzzaaaa…." – their slow chanting filled the room.

Images began to flash in front of his droopy eyelids. Dream Swap, the elixir of his life was in action now. He'd discovered this mystic mantra whilst roaming around an ancient tomb. It needed two willing partners and that's where Elena fit in.

Both had to see a dream at the same time, whilst chanting the mantra. But the dreams would come true only if the two individuals swapped them. She had to see something for him and vice-versa.

A papyrus lay folded on either side. Red ink defining what they were supposed to view. He'd narrated the scene to Elena atleast hundred times and there was no way she could go wrong with this. *'Aleksander stands in the balcony – his white robe fluttering as he waves to the sea of humanity below. The crown fits his head perfectly. He smiles triumphantly. He finally gets anointed as the pope of the Roman Catholic church.'*

Aleks, on the other hand wafted into a mutilated version of the dream Elena had written down for him. *'She crawls in the expanse of Albanian hinterland. She's all alone, coughing blood droplets on the white snow.'*

He woke up with a jerk, getting rid of her in the future. Elena was still dreaming, her pupils moving rapidly behind closed eyelashes.

After a few minutes, she woke up.

"I …." – he entered her in a rage of passion.

He no longer needed Elena, but why not enjoy her before she perishes.

"I loved you too…But"- she interrupted. "Dreaming for you and seeing what you want has killed my yearning for life."

"What are…"

"Let me complete, Aleks. I know that you've been altering my dreams"

"No, that's such a blasphemous allegation."

"Really! Over the last year, wasn't I fucked in your dreams by random boys? Your dreams eventually turned into my nightmares."

Aleks wasn't listening anymore.

"So here I am, a foolish love-stricken woman who is now nothing but a whore - with clientele ranging from the would-be pope to men similar to the ones, who raped you thirty years back."

He put on his cloak and peeped out the curtain. The street was desolate.

"But there will be retribution….Rudolph will crown you and…"

Her words trailed, as he stormed out. Why the hell did she have to add Rudolph in the dream. Now he was stuck with the plaintiff.

*   *   *

A crow cawed on the windowsill, staring at the feathers of his quill. He soaked it with ink as morning rays broke through the dark corner. 7 powerful clergymen, 7 subservient letters. *Pander to their egos and the seat is yours, Aleks*

Seasons changed colors, and Bishop Aleksander De Boer bid his time in the by lanes of his dying city. The time was set for a glorious turn of the century. His century.

Today, he awaited the big news. A monstrous rat gnawed the rug at his feet. The rodents had spread far and wide.

"How many people dead, Rudolph?"

"20 million, according to hearsay. This plague might see the end of Europe"

He looked out of the building, as clouds collided in the distance.

"This Black Death will see a new awakening."

"But sire, the pope…"

"Pour the wine, Rudolph….He will be dead tonight"

*   *   *

Aleks prayed as smoke rose from the Sistine Chapel chimney. A cardinal deacon, appeared on the terrace of St. Peter's Basilica and shouted "Habemus Papam!"

He was elected the 26th successor of St. Peter and leader of the worldwide Catholic Church consisting of more than 300 million followers.

Pope Aleksander de Boer stood in the balcony in fresh papal cassocks, waving to the sea of people below. The crown was big for his head – he smiled but felt a pang of loneliness. Emptiness. He hunched in the bitter cold, as snowflakes floated through. The Vatican was the universe with people filling in as stars.

He stood on a stool to be able to see the crowd better. He sensed someone approaching from behind. Before he could turn, a hand pushed him and he stumbled forwards. His robe hung on the nail near the edge, as he bobbed off the balcony. The crowd below started shouting.

"Aah…" - He looked up, his life hanging onto Rudolph's wrist.

An evil glint glowed in the plaintiff's eyes, as their hands started de-coupling. Rudolph released the grip and held a papyrus with red ink to his face.

Realization hit that Elena had altered the final dream and plotted this sequence with Rudolph a decade back.

"Surrogate revenge might be bitter, Aleks, but real revenge is definitely sweet!" "This black death will see a new awakening, indeed."

The robe tore off as he fell down rapidly, the quick fall snapping his spine into two. And a tear dropped from the balcony above. A tear of retribution.

> **'A dream you dream alone is only a dream.**
> **A dream you dream together is reality.'**
> **– John Lennon**

ACKNOWLEDGEMENTS

A big hug to mom and dad for allowing me to daydream through my formative years. Their love and the accompanying freedom have helped shape my thoughts. And to Vasudha for the balancing act of kicking me out of that stupor!

Also, a vote of thanks to Ruchika, Mihir, Mittali, Minal, Kedar and above all, Vasu again for their invaluable inputs to the original manuscript.

Finally, a shout-out to my chuddy buddies and other loved ones who've been a great support always. Max, Kulu, Rana, Pinks, Mittu, Vindisal, Himsi, Prachi, Pallo, Preethz, Officer, Pahadi, Akkimbo, Bawarchi, Bhavu, Nani, Ma, Pa, Neha, Didi, Sayla sisters and anyone I might have missed out – love you guys!

Sydney, Janine, Bon and the entire team at Partridge Publishing – thanks for your patience and helping get these stories out there, for posterity.